W9-CNR-784

I'm just a little sprout from a mighty spruce tree,
and I wonder—I wonder!—what will I be?

I don't know yet what I will be
or if there's something great in me.
But I will wait, and I will grow,
and one day, one year I will know.

Everybody's

TREE

Barbara Joosse

AND ILLUSTRATED BY *Renée Graef*

PUBLISHED BY SLEEPING BEAR PRESS™

I dig a hole for my little spruce tree,
then tuck in the roots of my little spruce tree.
I cover it with soil—
     a blanket soft and warm,
          snug-a-bug cozy—
a bed in the ground.

Hello again. Hello, old friend.
I brought someone special for you to meet—
someone tiny, someone new,
someone growing just like you.

Now there are grandbabies
still so small,
playing beside you,
grand and tall.

Our tree is old. Soon it will die.
Can we find a way to say goodbye?
Let's tie a ribbon for every year
our good friend has grown right here!

We fly through the *everywhere*,
searching for a tree—
ᴀ Christmas tree for *everybody*!
A sturdy spruce. Tall and wide.
A towering tree that
scrapes the sky.

We know it's hard to lose a tree.
We know it's part of your family.
But still ... will you share
with *everybody everywhere*?

We lower the crane to help the old tree down—
gently . . . gently . . . gently to the ground.
Then tie it down, snug and tight—
to keep it safe through the long, cool night.

We **creak** around the corner . . .
we **chug** up the hill . . .
we'll make it to the city–we will! We will!

Everybody shouts when we pass:
"Here's Everybody's Tree—at last! At last!"

We're **stringing, blinging,**
           ting-a-ling-a-linging!

We're stringing thousands of twinkle lights,
then crown with a star, glitter-star, glitter-night.

We **hurry**, **hurry**, **hurry**, getting ready to go,
getting ready for cold, getting ready for snow,
getting ready for *ooh!*, getting ready for *OH!*,
at the very merry, very derry
magical, fantastical CHRISTMAS TREE SHOW.

We gather all together—
all together, holding hands.
And we giggle and we jiggle,
and it's getting hard to stand.
And it's eight o'clock, it's late o'clock,
it's wait and wait and *wait o'clock*!

Oh, the cold, it is a-stinging
and the bells, they are a-ringing
and everybody's singing
for the lighting
oh tonight-ing
of Everybody's Tree!

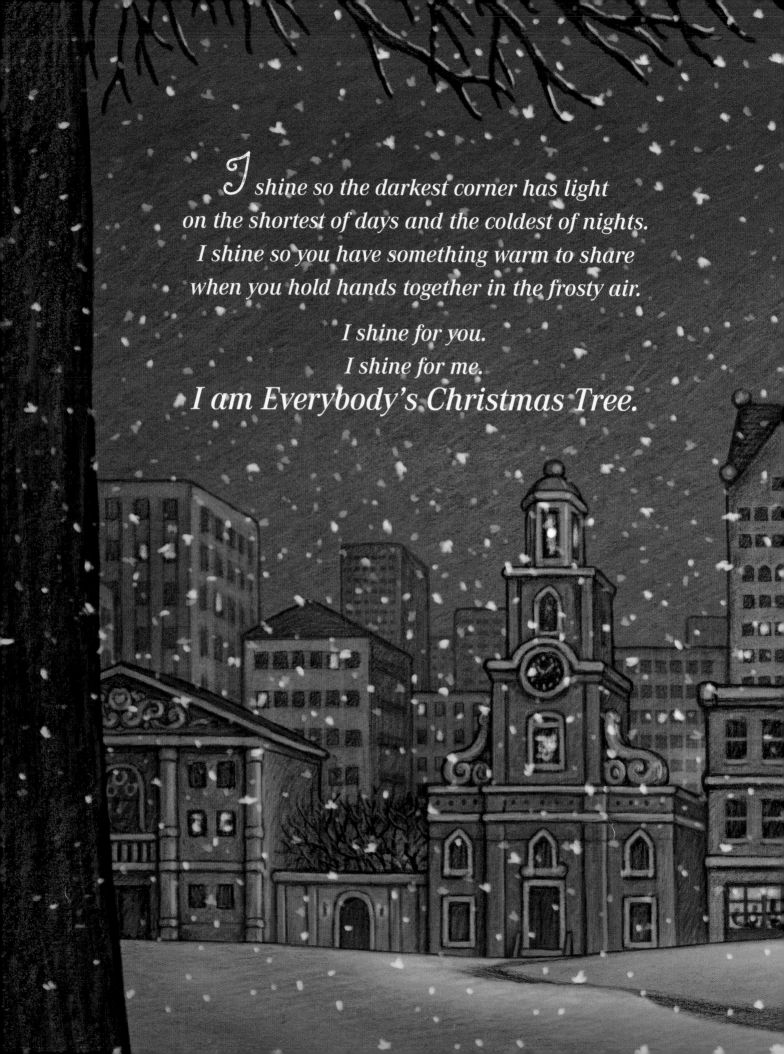

*I shine so the darkest corner has light
on the shortest of days and the coldest of nights.
I shine so you have something warm to share
when you hold hands together in the frosty air.*

*I shine for you.
I shine for me.*
I am Everybody's Christmas Tree.

To Leo and Micah,
the boys who make my heart smile
—Miss Barbara

For the beacons in my life who have lit the way:
My mom, Louise; my sister, Rhonda; and my husband, Bruce
—Renée

SLEEPING BEAR PRESS™

Text Copyright © 2020 Barbara Joosse • Illustration Copyright © 2020 Renée Graef
Design Copyright © 2020 Sleeping Bear Press • All rights reserved.
No part of this book may be reproduced in any manner without the express written consent of the publisher, except in the case of brief excerpts
in critical reviews and articles. All inquiries should be addressed to: Sleeping Bear Press • 2395 South Huron Parkway, Suite 200, Ann Arbor, MI 48104
www.sleepingbearpress.com © Sleeping Bear Press • Printed and bound in the United States. • 10 9 8 7 6 5 4 3

Library of Congress Cataloging-in-Publication Data • Names: Joosse, Barbara M., author. • Graef, Renée, illustrator. • Title: Everybody's tree / Barbara Joosse ; and illustrated by Renée Graef.
Description: Ann Arbor, MI : Sleeping Bear Press, [2020] • Audience: Ages 4-8. • Summary: "Over the course of eighty years a spruce tree grows, along with the little boy who first selected it at a tree farm. At the
end of its life, the tree is chosen to be the centerpiece of a city's holiday celebration"– Provided by publisher. • Identifiers: LCCN 2020006341 • ISBN 9781534110588 (hardcover) • Subjects: CYAC: Stories in rhyme.
Trees–Fiction. • Christmas–Fiction. • Classification: LCC PZ8.3.J756 Ex 2020 • DDC [E]–dc23 • LC record available at https://lccn.loc.gov/2020006341